I Love You BECAUSE I Love You

Words by **Mượn Thị Văn**   Art by **Jessica Love**

KATHERINE TEGEN BOOKS
An Imprint of HarperCollins Publishers

Katherine Tegen Books is an imprint of HarperCollins Publishers.

I Love You Because I Love You

Text copyright © 2022 by Mượn Thị Văn

Illustrations copyright © 2022 by Jessica Love

All rights reserved. Manufactured in Italy.

No part of this book may be used or reproduced in any manner whatsoever without written permission except in the case of brief

quotations embodied in critical articles and reviews. For information address HarperCollins Children's Books,

a division of HarperCollins Publishers, 195 Broadway, New York, NY 10007.

www.harpercollinschildrens.com

ISBN 978-0-06-289459-5

The artist used a brush, acrylic ink, watercolor, and gouache on Stonehenge "Faun" paper to create her illustrations.

Typography by Dana Fritts

21 22 23 24 25 RTLO 10 9 8 7 6 5 4 3 2 1

❖

First Edition

I love you because
you know when I'm sad.

Because I love you, no mistake is ever too great.

I love you because
you let me make mistakes.

Because I love you,
food tastes better when shared.

I love you because
you cook with care.

Because I love you,
love blooms where our voices meet.

I love you because you let me speak.

Because I love you, I see more than before.

I love you because you see what others miss.

Because I love you,
the world becomes
our playground.

I love you because
you play with me.

Because I love you, I am strong.

I love you because you carry me.

Because I love you, I am here.

And I love you because you're here.

because you're you.

I love you because . . .

To my family.

—M.T.V.

To my mom & dad:

I love you.

—J.L.

Because I love you,
I share the good with the bad.

I love you because
you're brave when I'm afraid.

Because I love you,
I am braver every day.

I love you because
you wait for me.

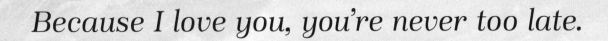

Because I love you, you're never too late.

I love you because you tell the best stories.

Because I love you,
my best story is you.

I love you because we go together.

Because I love you, we change and grow together.

I love you because . . .